D1637693

The Emperor's Gruckle Hound

Kathryn Cave

Illustrated by
Chris Riddell

h
Hodder
Children's
Books

a division of Hodder Headline plc

First published in Great Britain in 1996
by Hodder Children's Books

A Catalogue record for this book is available from
the British Library

ISBN 0 340 65599 2

Typeset by Avon Dataset Ltd, Bidford-on-Avon

Printed and bound in Great Britain by
Cox & Wyman Ltd, Reading, Berks

Hodder Children's Books
a division of Hodder Headline plc
338 Euston Road
London NW1 3BH

For Helena and Alasdair

Chapter One

Once upon a time there were two puppies.

They were born behind a row of dustbins in a backyard criss-crossed with washing-lines that served a dozen houses. They belonged to no one.

Their mother was thin and hungry. She lived on what she could beg or steal, dodging stones and kicks and wheels through the long, hot days of August. When September came, she explained to the puppies that soon they would have to look after themselves. One frosty October morning, she trotted out into the street and never came back.

That night, the puppies shivered in their home behind the dustbins. When at last the city began to stir, they crept out to find something to eat . . .

It was the Emperor's birthday. Everyone who mattered had been racking their brains for weeks over what to give him.

He had everything a man could possibly want (and most of the things no one could possibly want), but every year on the third of October, the top people in the city streamed up the Avenue of Seven Victories to give him an awful lot more. Schools and shops shut in honour of the occasion, so a lot of ordinary people who had nothing better to do came to the square in front of the palace to watch: butchers, bakers, candlestick-makers, clerks and accountants, waiters and waitresses, ice-cream men and hot-dog sellers . . .

Tucked in among the throng was a tinker called Gregory, who had his hands full fighting a losing battle with his daughter Anna.

'No,' he said firmly. He'd been saying the same for the past ten minutes, ever since she'd found the stray puppy whimpering behind a dustbin, and scooped it up. 'You can't keep it. You know you can't keep it. You've already got a cat and that horrible pigeon. Isn't that enough for you?'

Anna was small and scruffy, with brown eyes

and a very determined chin. 'Tom and Arnold aren't mine. They just visit. A puppy would be different. He'd always be here.'

'I don't want him always to be here,' her father said frankly. 'I want him *never* to be here. I mean, look at him! He's . . . he's . . . Words fail me, Anna – he's that bad. Put him down before you get fleas.'

She held on. 'He'd be company for me. You know how late you come home. And he'd frighten burglars.'

'Burglars?' Gregory repeated, stunned. 'What have we got for a burglar to steal? And if we had anything, what could *that* do to stop him? Make him die laughing? And what would he eat?'

'How should I know what burglars eat?' Anna growled, holding the puppy closer.

'I meant the dog,' her father said, 'as you very well know.'

'He's only little. He'll hardly eat anything. And he probably won't live very long because I think his paw's broken.' The gruff voice trembled.

'What?' Gregory frowned. 'Let me see. Just because he limps, it doesn't mean his leg's broken. And if it was, it wouldn't kill him. Broken bones mend. The pigeon's wing mended, didn't it?' He ran his hand gently down the puppy's leg. 'It's just bruised. It'll be as good as new in a day or two. Put him down now. It's time we went home and had lunch.'

Anna looked at him. 'He can sleep on my bed,' she said, as if that solved everything.

'No!' Gregory shouted. 'Not *on* your bed, *under* it. And that's my final offer.' When she had stopped hugging him, he said: 'So, what shall we call the scruffy creature? Filth? Fleabag? It's going to be a difficult decision.'

Anna thought. 'Scruff!' she said at last. 'Let's call him Scruff.'

They set off down the Avenue of Seven Victories towards home.

By twelve-thirty, people were leaving their presents on the palace steps. By two, the presents had spilled over into the square in front of the palace. There were huge things, like the full-size bronze rhinoceros that took six strong men to carry it, and tiny ones like the history of Algernon the Awful, the Emperor's grandfather, written on rice paper and bound into a book that would fit into the palm of your hand. There were things to eat, things to wear, things to hang on the wall in a dark corner. There were spiky things, slippery things, knobbly things, and things so peculiar that no one knew what they were or which way up to put them. And still the presents kept coming.

At three o'clock, the Emperor's chief advisor, Lord Hawk, issued an order that every man, woman and boy who worked in the palace was to stop what they were doing and come and carry in presents instead. Cleaners stopped cleaning, footmen stopped footling, kitchen boys stopped peeling potatoes and chopping onions, and, in the palace gardens, Fred – the youngest and least important of the assistant gardener's assistants – stopped trimming the grass with a pair of shears the size of nail scissors, and heaved a sigh of relief.

Ten minutes later you could have found him, whistling cheerfully, in the square in front of the palace, stuffing peaches into a silver vase. When the vase was full, he tossed a silk nightshirt over one shoulder, heaved a bale of hay up on top of his head, and hoisted a porcelain dinner service under one arm.

'Don't,' said a junior footman, carrying a parrot in a cage shaped like the dome of St Paul's. 'You'll come a cropper. And Hawk-Eye won't like it.' He jerked his head towards the door where Lord Hawk loomed with an enormous clip-board.

Fred lobbed a hamper into the air and grinned as he fielded it neatly on top of the bale of hay. 'Have a bit of faith, Carl. The more we carry, the quicker we finish. I can do this with my eyes shut.'

'Don't say I didn't warn you.' Carl set off

for the steps, and then looked back: 'And watch out for the puppy.'

The hay had sagged down round Fred's ears. 'What?' he said. 'I can't hear you.'

'A stray puppy,' Carl repeated patiently. 'Over by the steps. Almost tripped Paul up just now.'

Fred grinned. 'Can't hear a word. Good thing you never say anything worth listening to, isn't it?' He set off for the steps.

'Oh dear,' Carl said gently thirty seconds later. 'Told you.'

Fred sat up and shook his head. He hoped that what he was seeing was a rare side-effect of hitting his head on a concrete step, but he was afraid it wasn't.

The Emperor's presents lay all around him.

One hundred interestingly shattered dinner plates. One seriously squashed silver vase with a light dressing of pulped peaches. One ripped purple nightshirt that— Fred blinked. One ripped purple nightshirt that was doing its best to be somewhere else?

He stooped, groped gingerly under the billowing silk, and found himself holding—

'A puppy!' He looked down in astonishment. 'You're what tripped me up, are you? Hey, stop wriggling, I won't hurt you. Where did you come from, eh?'

The puppy shivered and licked his hand. It was so thin that he could feel every bone in its body. 'You want some food,' he said softly. 'What can we find you? Aha!'

The ham had fallen out of its hamper, rolled down the steps, and come to rest in a puddle. Looking casually at the sky, Fred kicked the

15

ham deftly behind one of the marble lions that flanked the steps, and then ducked down out of sight.

'Here, mate!' He carved a neat helping with his penknife as he spoke. 'Eat up. Reckon you need it more than most.'

'*What* is this mess?' an awful voice rang out from the top of the steps. '*Which* idiot is responsible?'

'Uh-oh!' Clutching the cut side of ham to his chest, Fred scrambled to his feet. 'Me, my lord, sorry my lord. I tripped.' Out of the corner of his eye he could see the puppy's tail wagging as it tucked in.

Lord Hawk shut his eyes. 'I might have known. Why is it *always* you? Clear this mess up at once and get back to work, idiot.'

'Yes, my lord.' For the next hour Fred scurried up and down the steps, too busy to do more than snatch a glance towards the marble lion, but whenever he looked, the puppy was still there.

'Forget about it,' Carl advised as they loaded up again side by side. 'The old bird's in a terrible temper. Half the presents have lost their labels, and you know how upset he gets about that.'

'If only I could take him in with me . . .' Fred said, not listening. 'It'll be cold tonight. Feel that wind? He needs warmth, and food, and looking after.'

A gust of wind raced across the square, scouring dead leaves and dust into the boys' faces. Something whisked out from behind the statue of Algernon the Awful, and wound itself round Fred's right ankle. It was a length of plaited gold and silver cord, with a label at one end:

To Our Beloved Emperor
From the Guild for the Preservation
of Rare and Exotic Beasts

'Uh-oh, another missing label! Wonder what that came off?' Fred wound the cord into a coil, and stuffed it into the pocket he kept Useful Things in, on top of a blue glass marble and a twig that looked like a person.

'Who knows what it came off? Who cares?' Carl reached into the heap of presents and grabbed a felt hat like a coal-scuttle decorated with pigeon feathers. 'You can't tell a present by its label. Come on, I'm freezing.'

17

Fred stayed where he was, one hand in his pocket. His face had a strange expression.

'What's the matter now?' Carl asked. 'Not having another of your brainwaves, are you?' Fred's brainwaves were famous throughout the palace. 'Like the one last week about growing runner beans instead of roses in the courtyard?' He chuckled. 'Or the one yesterday, about turning the big flower-bed into a wild-life reserve? I hear the Head Gardener loved that!'

'Shh!' Fred's eyes had a far-away look. 'I'm . . . I'm *thinking*.'

'Don't,' said Carl for the second time. 'Your sort of thinking means trouble.'

For the second time that day, he was absolutely right.

'Name?' snapped Lord Hawk at Fred five minutes later. 'And don't say "Frederick" this time, boy. I have no interest in your name, merely the name of the donor.'

'Guild for the Preservation of Rare and Exotic Beasts, my lord,' Fred rattled out.

'Present?'

'One hamper, woven. One beast, exotic. I'll put them in the drawing-room, shall I?' He

18

kept the hamper as far as possible from Lord Hawk.

'Wait!' Lord Hawk looked up with a frown. 'Beast is not good enough. We cannot write to thank the Guild for a *beast*. What sort of beast is it?'

Fred lifted the lid of the hamper and peered inside. 'Er, well . . . it's small and sort of browny grey, and it looks a bit like a dog, my lord.' He let the lid fall and gave Lord Hawk his most winning smile.

The smile was wasted. Lord Hawk sighed heavily and reached out for the hamper. One glance inside and his eyebrows snapped down.

'A bit like a dog? This isn't a *bit* like a dog, boy. It's a *lot* like a dog. In fact, it *is* a dog. Why on earth have the Guild chosen to give the Emperor this revolting-looking dog?'

'It's a very rare dog, my lord,' Fred answered. 'Look what the label says.'

The occupant of the basket – small, grubby, and painfully thin – wore a collar of plaited gold and silver cord from which a label dangled. The front of it said:

To Our Beloved Emperor
From the Guild for the Preservation
of Rare and Exotic Beasts

There was another message on the back:

tHe LaSt oF thE GrUckLe HoUndS
pLeaSe FeEd ReGulArLy

Lord Hawk's frown
grew deeper. 'Gruckle
hounds? *Gruckle*
hounds?'

'They're from Austria, my lord,' Fred said helpfully. 'My gran told me about them. They live in the mountains and they hunt gruckles. That's why they're called gruckle hounds.'

If there's one thing an Emperor's advisor hates, it's being told things by someone like Fred. Lord Hawk's glare would have withered a bed of marigolds. 'I know that! Do you think I don't know what a gruckle hound is?'

'Oh! Sorry, my lord!' Fred sounded very humble. 'They're very rare and exotic, and not in any of the books. Lots of people haven't heard of them.'

This time Lord Hawk's glare would have shrivelled a clump of oak trees. 'Well I *have*. Why didn't you say it was a gruckle hound in the first place? Take it to the drawing-room with the other presents and get back to work.'

'Yes, my lord,' Fred said obediently. 'Sorry, my lord.'

It was all he could do not to dance along the marble corridor.

He bumped into Carl at the drawing-room door. 'Meet the gruckle hound,' he announced, flourishing the hamper. 'I'm calling him Sam. He looks like a Sam, doesn't he?'

The puppy stood up on its hind legs and peered over the rim, wagging its tail so hard that it seemed to be wagging its whole body.

Carl stared at it. 'The *what*?'

Fred winked and gave him a dig in the ribs. 'Don't tell me you've never heard of a gruckle hound! Lord Hawk knows about them, even though they're not in any of the books. But then, old Hawk-Eye knows everything.'

Carl looked from Sam to his friend and slowly shook his head. 'If you mean what I think you mean, you've really done it. When he finds out, he'll have you skinned alive.'

'Why should he find out?' Fred answered. 'It's not as if the Emperor *keeps* his presents. He'll give Sam away, like the rest. And whoever gets him will look after him, because he comes from the Emperor! How's Hawk-Eye ever going to find out he's not the last of the gruckle hounds after all?'

'He will, that's all,' said the voice of experience. 'He just will.'

Chapter Two

Scruff took his first bath under the cold tap in the yard. He made such a noise that windows were thrown open and heads stuck out all down the street.

'Stop wriggling!' Gregory cried, wrestling with a puppy as wet and slippery as a fish. 'I've got you now! No, you don't! Ouch! Don't stand there laughing, Anna: catch him!'

She did her best, but it's hard to catch a wet puppy hell-bent on tearing round in circles at high speed. Particularly if you can't stop laughing.

'Got you!' she gasped at last, sitting down in a puddle with the puppy clasped to her chest. 'Look at you, you bad dog! You're dirtier than ever.'

He licked her nose.

'So are you.' Gregory leant against the wall

and wiped his eyes. 'You'd better go under the tap too. Maybe if you hold him he won't mind so much. But whatever you do, don't let go.'

'*I* didn't let him go last time,' she pointed out with dignity. 'Come on, Scruff. We'll have a bath together. You'll like it, won't you?'

She couldn't have been more wrong.

It was past midnight, but the lights still blazed in the drawing-room at the palace, where the Emperor was glumly inspecting his haul of presents. How on earth was he going to get rid of them without offending people?

Groceries and clothing went to the poor, of course. Sweets and cakes could go to the children's hospital. But where could he send a set of underpants studded with diamond spikes like pigeon's claws, or a stone pillow that was meant to cure chicken pox and the fear of hedgehogs?

To the mad house?

He turned wearily to his advisor. 'You know everything, Hawk: what would my father have done?'

'Auctioned them for charity,' said Lord

Hawk without hesitation.

'Wonderful.' The Emperor sighed. 'What would I do without you? Thank everyone very much and auction the rest of the presents for charity. Could you introduce a law to abolish birthdays?'

'I doubt it, your highness.' Lord Hawk consulted the clipboard. 'That leaves just the livestock to dispose of. One timber wolf, one leopard with mange, one parrot minus feathers, one crocodile, two lizards, one performing python, and one gruckle hound.'

'One gruckle hound?' the Emperor asked with a flicker of interest. 'What's that?'

'An Austrian mountain dog, your highness,' said Lord Hawk smoothly. 'It hunts.'

'Hunts what?'

'Gruckles, your highness, naturally.'

'Oh, naturally,' the Emperor said quickly. 'Just so. Gruckles.' He wished he knew what a gruckle was, but he'd have died rather than ask right out. 'Dangerous work, is it, gruckle-hunting?'

Lord Hawk smiled. 'The risks are considerable, but in my experience there is no sport to match it, none at all.'

The Emperor blinked. 'You've done it yourself? Actually hunted gruckles? With a gruckle hound?'

There was a pause of perhaps a thousandth of a second. 'Long ago,' Lord Hawk said modestly. 'One must be fit, your highness. It is a young man's sport.'

'I see, I see.' The most exciting thing the Emperor had ever done was take tennis lessons, and Lord Hawk had made him give those up when he got a sore elbow. 'And you need a gruckle hound to do it?'

'It is essential,' Lord Hawk said crisply. 'And, of course, they are now extremely rare. Your gruckle hound is thought to be the last of its kind.' He looked grave. 'It is a solemn thought.'

The Emperor tried to look grave too, but only succeeded in looking depressed. 'It's an awful responsibility. What should I do with it? Is it big? Perhaps I ought to inspect it. The last of the gruckle hounds . . .' The phrase had rather a ring to it. Suddenly the Emperor made up his mind. 'I *will* see it. When you think, Hawk, it's nothing short of a . . . a sacred trust.'

'My sentiments exactly.' Lord Hawk reached for the tasselled bell-pull. 'I will have the animal fetched at once.'

Anna found a sweater that had shrunk, and made Scruff a nest in a box under her bed. He chewed up the box, retrieved the sweater, and laid it lovingly at her slippered feet.

'*Good* dog!' Anna said, much impressed.

Gregory looked at the puppy with a more jaundiced eye. 'Yes, I agree he could be telling us he doesn't want to sleep in a box,' he said, bleary-eyed, an hour later. 'You may even be right in saying he's intelligent, although I can't see much sign of it myself. All *I'm* saying is that he's noisy. It's past midnight! He'll get the street a bad name.'

He broke off as a battered black cat with half an ear missing sprang up on to the window-sill and scratched the glass. 'And that cat will definitely get us a bad name.' He shook his head as Anna pushed up the sash. 'They've got Wanted posters up for him all over town. Don't tell me you let him in every night?' He groaned as a huge pigeon lumbered down from the chimney-pot and waddled in through

28

the window on the cat's heels. 'And that horrible bird as well? They're as bad as each other. The biggest thieves in the city,' he finished with feeling.

Anna pulled down the window. 'They'll keep Scruff company. Make him feel at home. Stop him being lonely. You know.'

'Teach him bad habits, more likely,' her father said shrewdly as he switched out the light. He switched it on again to remind her: 'And they sleep *under* the bed, remember.'

'Well, where else would they go?' she asked in a pitying voice.

Before Fred came to the palace, he lived with his gran in a poky room behind an ironmonger's shop. One of the bad things about his job was not being allowed to live with her any more. Now he had an equally poky room on the top floor of the palace. It was too hot in summer, too cold in winter, and every time he stood up he hit his head on the ceiling.

It was a start, though, he told himself as he lay down. He wouldn't always be an assistant gardener's assistant. One day he'd become an assistant gardener, and then a gardener, and then – who knows? – maybe Head Gardener himself. A boy could dream, couldn't he?

His dreams were rudely interrupted at one-thirty by Carl shaking his shoulder.

'Wake up! They want the gruckle hound – the Emperor and Hawk-Eye! Is it up here?'

'*Gruckle* hound?' Fred rubbed his eyes. A damp nose prodded him in the small of his back. 'Ow! Oh, I remember. Yes, he's here.'

'Get dressed and bring him down pronto if you know what's good for you,' Carl said grimly. '*You're* going to show him to the Emperor. *I'm* not, not for anything.'

'Why do they want him?' Fred asked from inside his shirt. 'Do you think they—' a button flew off as his head popped out '—suspect anything?'

'How should I know?' Carl cried. 'Do you suppose the Emperor would tell me. "Oh Carl, just pop off and get the so-called gruckle hound so I can check no one's pulling my imperial leg"? All I can say is that anyone with half a brain would suspect something! You can't take an ordinary puppy and persuade the world it's an exotic beast no one's heard of. People aren't that stupid!'

'He's not ordinary,' Fred said mildly as he pulled on his boots.

'He's not a gruckle hound either!'

'But he's a really quick learner. He knows his name, and I've almost taught him to sit. And when he made a puddle you could tell he was sorry. All he needs is a bit of love and attention and he'll be brilliant.'

'Fat chance he'll get much love and attention here when Hawk-Eye finds out the truth,' Carl said tersely. 'A boot on the backside and out into the street, that's what he'll get then. And so will you, most likely.

Hurry up!'

'I'm ready.' Fred scooped the puppy off the bed and placed him gently back in the basket. 'Better make sure no one finds out then, hadn't we?'

'So this is the gruckle hound . . .' The Emperor peered curiously at Sam, who was sitting shivering on the marble floor. 'I would never have guessed. Would you have guessed it was a gruckle hound, Hawk?'

Fred held his breath as the Emperor's advisor flicked a speck of dust from his cuff. He let it out again as Lord Hawk spoke:

'At this age the breed looks unremarkable, your highness, but a true expert can tell. The shape of the head is unmistakable.'

'The head . . .' The Emperor stared down at the puppy with narrowed eyes. 'Y-e-e-s, I think I see what you mean. And I suppose it will look quite different when it grows up?' He turned inquiringly to Fred.

'Not . . . not *that* different, your highness.' Fred was startled to discover that it felt worse lying to him than it did to Lord Hawk.

'Bigger though?' the Emperor insisted.

Fred hesitated, wrestling with his conscience.

'Naturally,' Lord Hawk said impatiently.

'And fierce?'

'We-e-e-ll . . .'

'Like a tiger, your highness,' said Lord Hawk. 'As any gruckle-hunter will testify.'

The puppy yawned and laid its head down on Fred's boot.

'He doesn't *look* fierce,' the Emperor said perceptively.

'They don't normally.' Fred got over his attack of conscience with a rush. 'Only when there're gruckles about.'

'Quite,' Lord Hawk said loudly, unwilling to let Fred hog the limelight. 'And then . . .'

'Then they bristle from head to toe,' Fred said. 'And they . . . they growl something horrible. Grrr!'

The Emperor shied away.

'And then . . . they spring!' Lord Hawk's imitation of a gruckle hound in action surprised everyone, including himself. 'And they rip the gruckle to shreds! Your highness,' he added more quietly.

'Until there's nothing left but its deadly gruckle-horn!' Fred finished in triumph. 'And its cruel claws, and its *enormous* teeth.'

'Good heavens!' The Emperor quietly abandoned any thought of gruckle-hunting. 'What an extraordinary creature it must be. And it looks so peaceful sleeping there . . . You know what, Hawk? I'll keep it! The last of the gruckle hounds . . . It can be my mascot. I can hardly wait to see what it's like when it grows up.'

Fred's stomach turned a double somersault

and sunk into his boots.

'Don't gape, boy,' Lord Hawk said sharply. 'Remove the gruckle hound. It must go to the imperial kennels for training tomorrow! The Emperor has spoken.'

Scruff was asleep, with his head on Anna's stomach, an arrangement equally satisfying to both. Untroubled by their gentle snores, the cat and pigeon discussed the new arrival.

Not bad, was the cat's verdict, *considering. He's got spirit. Might turn out well. Needs training, of course.*

The pigeon bobbed his head. *Begging or stealing?*

Both. Nothing to beat a good general education. Will you propose the motion, or shall I? The cat yawned and performed an elaborate stretch. *I hereby propose that the new recruit starts full training first thing tomorrow. Agreed?*

Agreed, the pigeon nodded.

Chapter Three

When Sam came back to the palace, he was every inch an Emperor's dog. He knew how to greet a foreign ambassador (one soft bark) or a head of state (two). He could march in a state procession, as proud as any general. He could snooze through a ballet, or stand like a statue for hours on the parade ground, even when bored, or cold, or tired.

He didn't share Fred's tiny room any longer, naturally. The Emperor's gruckle hound slept on a silk cushion in a kennel outside the Emperor's own door. Each morning, a junior footman gave him a perfumed bath, dried him with a velvet towel, and brought him breakfast on a jewelled plate.

'He's changed!' Fred complained bitterly when Carl led him out into the courtyard one breezy May morning. 'He's forgotten how to

play. Look at him!'

A butterfly landed on Sam's ear. Instead of shaking his head, like any normal dog, Sam tried to pretend it didn't exist. He had to concentrate so hard he looked as if he was doing long division sums in his head.

'They've ruined him with their training. He behaves like a . . . like a . . .' For once Fred found himself lost for words.

'Like a gruckle hound?' his friend suggested mildly. 'That's what he's meant to be, remember? The less he carries on like other dogs, the better for him and the better for you. It's a pity he doesn't grow faster, or look more fierce. Someone's bound to twig sooner or later. It's just a matter of time.' Carl was always saying things like that.

'Some gruckle hounds take years to reach full size,' Fred said quickly. 'They're what-d'you-call-it: slow developers.'

Carl grinned. 'Pull the other one. It's me you're talking to, the one who knows. And make up your mind,' he added, 'what you expect him to be: the last of the gruckle hounds or a regular puppy. Because he can't be both.'

'Why not?' Fred cried. 'Why should he have to be the last of something before people care about him? Ordinary animals matter just as much. I'm beginning to wish I'd never said he was something he's not.'

'Well, you did,' Carl reminded him. 'And you're stuck with it, both of you. I warned you, didn't I?'

Fred was too fed up to answer.

A week later the Emperor gave one of his regular evening concerts. Sam sat to attention beside the throne, lost in the music. When it was over, Carl let him out to walk in the courtyard.

Fred was at work on his hands and knees, polishing each slab of stone until it shone in the moonlight. Sam sniffed the air gravely, in a manner befitting the last of the gruckle hounds, when all of a sudden something floated down on to his nose.

Startled, he shook his head and barked. *Hey, you!* the bark said. *See to this!*

Fred looked over his shoulder. 'What's the matter, your dogginess? A sycamore leaf? In the Emperor's courtyard? What an outrage!'

Absolutely, Sam thought. *Couldn't agree more.*

Fred put the leaf in his pocket, and scratched Sam's glossy head. 'Don't tell me you haven't seen a leaf fall off a tree before? What else are you missing out on, mate?' He went on scratching the dog's head. 'Puddles? Rain? Cats? Other dogs? Life's not much fun for you, is it?'

Fun? Sam stood like a statue. He liked having his head scratched. All the same, he was deeply offended.

He saw plenty of dogs through the window of the Emperor's car when they went for drives. He knew about rain too from seeing how wet the footmen got carrying the umbrellas on official occasions. As for fun . . .

I'm not meant to have fun, Sam thought indignantly. *I'm far too important. Surely even a gardener's boy ought to know that?*

Not this one, apparently. 'Hey!' he cried, eyes lighting up. 'I know how to give you some fun! Hang on a tick.'

Sam sighed. *Now what?*

Fred dived off in the direction of the toolshed. A moment later he was back, cobwebs trailing from his hair, with a small blue ball.

Sam sniffed it and turned away. *What does he take me for – a puppy?*

Fred crossed his eyes to watch a tiny spider parachute off his forehead. 'Come on,' he said coaxingly to Sam when it had landed safely. 'I throw the ball and you run after it, right?'

Sam looked at him in disbelief. *Run? A dog in my position?*

'Don't look like that. You'll love it, I bet! Here goes: *Fetch!*'

He threw the ball, and it bounced into a fountain.

Good grief! Sam stalked deliberately in the opposite direction and sat down on one of the stones Fred had polished. *I'm going to pretend this whole ridiculous business never happened,* he sniffed.

Fred still didn't get the message. A few seconds later, he was back again. 'You've got one last chance, your dogginess,' he said gravely. Water trickled down his sleeve on to the stones from where he'd fished the ball out of the fountain. 'See this ball? It's yours if you fetch it. I bet they taught you how to fetch at the kennels. You haven't forgotten, have you?'

Sam stiffened, and gave Fred a cold look. *Forgotten? A gruckle hound never forgets.*

'Here goes then: *Fetch!*'

Somehow, and Sam wasn't at all sure himself how it happened, when Fred hurled the ball, Sam hurled himself after it. Only this time it bounced over the wall and into the street.

Sam put the brakes on too late, skidded into the wall and banged his nose. *Ouch!*

Fred let out a cry of dismay. The gate to the street was locked at sunset. There was no way to get the ball back.

He scratched Sam's head again. 'Sorry, your dogginess. You'll have to wait. Tomorrow somebody's bound to send me out into the city. I'll get your ball then, honest.'

What do you mean, tomorrow? Sam stalked over to the gate and barked once. *I want it NOW.*

'No hope.' An earwig shot into orbit as Fred shook his head. 'I told you: you'll have to wait. Here's Carl come to get you. Goodnight, your woofiness!'

Lying in his kennel that night, Sam thought about the ball. When he shut his eyes he could see it sailing through air. If it hadn't been for the wall, he might have caught it.

He *wanted* to catch it.

Was catching something gruckle hounds did? It must be, Sam thought, *or I wouldn't want it so much. And now I'm meant to wait – wait! – until Fred finds time to get it back for me!*

It was months since Sam had had to wait for anything. He didn't like it.

That boy should show more respect, he told himself, laying his nose on his paws. *I'm not just any dog. I'm the last of the gruckle hounds. If I want my ball, I'll . . . I'll . . .*

He wasn't quite sure what he'd do, until a wonderful idea came to him.

I'll go and get it myself!

Chapter Four

'Keep that dog in today,' Gregory told Anna as he reached for his coat after breakfast. Scruff looked up from the bone he was gnawing under the table. 'There've been complaints.'

Anna was making a mobile on the kitchen table out of bits of bent wire and silver foil. She didn't look up. 'The butcher?'

'And others.' Gregory grinned. 'That red-headed thug who hangs about by the river claims Scruff bit him.'

'Good,' Anna growled. 'He throws stones at cats. I've seen him.'

'And Alf Fishguard—'

'*He* sets traps for birds. He's a horrible man.'

'A horrible man who, thanks to Scruff, needs a patch on the seat of his trousers. Lucky he hasn't worked out yet who owns the dog that bit him. Then there's Mrs Hubble, who left a pork chop on the table by the open window—'

'What does she expect, leaving food lying around?' Anna pushed back her fringe and scowled at her father. 'And how does she know it was Scruff who took it?'

'Oh, Scruff didn't take it,' Gregory said cheerfully. 'A cat took it. She saw the whole thing. The cat hooked it off the table and swatted it into the yard—'

'There you are, then,' Anna began, much relieved.

'—where it was picked up by a mongrel answering Scruff's description,' Gregory continued. 'The dog ran off but according to Mrs Hubble she'd have caught him, if it hadn't been for the pigeon.'

Anna dropped the mobile. 'A pigeon?' she asked, rather red in the face when she'd finished gathering up the pieces.

'Yes, apparently it dive-bombed her until she retreated inside. Curious story, isn't it?' Her father took a last gulp of coffee. 'Reminds me of one I heard last week. There was this butcher who opened his shop door because

45

he heard a dog howling. As soon as the door was open, a pigeon flew in and snatched a pack of sliced salami from the counter. He was trying to stun the bird with a broom, when he tripped over—' he looked mildly at his daughter. 'What was it he tripped over, Anna?'

'A cat?' Anna suggested gruffly, frowning at the mobile.

'Quite right, a cat. In the confusion, all three animals vanished. Along with the pack of salami, half a dozen sausages, and a piece of pig's liver. It's an intriguing story.' The tinker patted his pockets to check he had his tools. 'A cat, a dog and a pigeon . . . It's the sort of thing you remember, isn't it?'

Anna grunted.

'So keep Scruff in today,' Gregory finished gently, 'and give everyone a chance to forget. Do I get a goodbye hug, or are you too busy?'

He had his hug, and left.

And since he didn't quite shut the door behind him, five minutes later, so did Scruff.

How does a dog set about retrieving a ball from outside the palace when he's never allowed out unattended? During a five-course lunch, Sam considered the problem from every angle.

So far as he could see, there was only one solution.

When he went out to the courtyard after lunch, Fred ruffled his hair in a highly disrespectful fashion. He'd just been given an exciting piece of news.

'Guess who's leading you in the parade this afternoon?' he demanded. 'Me, that's who! Carl's got a cold, and Mike's sick, and Ben's sprained his ankle, and grumpy Giles is visiting his grandma, and everyone else is too important, so I'm the only one left. What do you think of that, eh? We're going to go walkies!'

Sam put up unusually well with having his hair ruffled all over again.

So Fred was going to be holding the lead that afternoon? Good.

Better than good, in fact.

Perfect.

'Scruff? *Scruff!*'

Anna turned the house upside down in the hope of finding the dog asleep under her bed or behind the sofa. Then she searched the yard, which didn't take long, and after that the alley.

She spotted Arnold having a dust-bath.

She passed Tom, asleep on a sunny window-sill.

But there was no sign at all of a scruffy small dog with a habit of putting his head on one side when deeply interested.

'Scruff!' Anna shouted crossly. 'Where are you?'

'Don't smile, boy.' Lord Hawk looked Fred up and down with a pained expression. 'Escorting the gruckle hound is a great responsibility. Do you understand?'

'Yes, my lord,' said Fred, very solemn.

'What's wrong with your trousers?'

'They're Carl's, my lord. I'm taller than him. It doesn't show if I pull my socks up.'

'Pull them up, then!' Lord Hawk snapped. 'And straighten the gruckle hound's ribbon. This isn't a circus. Right! Now take your place in the line, behind the Emperor's carriage. And remember – *I* will be watching you. Proceed!'

The square in front of the palace was filled with people cheering and waving flags.

'Hear that?' Fred muttered to Sam as they marched down the Avenue of Seven Victories. 'They're cheering us – you and me, your dogginess!'

Just me, actually, Sam corrected mildly.

As they walked past, a group of school-children started showering them with confetti. Fred beamed and waved at them graciously. 'The city is ours!' he chortled. 'Why don't we do something really special for everyone – lay on a public holiday or something, eh?'

Sam allowed his tail to twitch, which was the nearest a gruckle hound ever comes to wagging it. He had something special in mind too, as it happened. Only it wasn't going to be what Fred expected.

Five minutes later, when the brass band was playing its loudest, and the crowd all around was shouting and cheering and waving banners, he tugged the lead from Fred's hand, slipped through the legs of a four-star general, and darted into the crowd.

'Hey!' Fred cried, coming down to earth with a jolt. 'Come back!'

'Idiot!' the Lord Chamberlain hissed
without moving his lips as he stalked past. 'Get
the gruckle hound back or you're . . .'

A fanfare of trumpets drowned the next
word, but something told Fred it was 'sacked'.

'I said *come back!*' he shouted, diving into
the crowd.

Sam padded briskly along the pavement,

head high, the golden lead trailing behind him. So far so good. All he had to do was find his way to the street behind the palace. He stopped at the first corner to sniff the breeze and decide which way to go.

Fred caught sight of the purple ribbon for a moment and let out a yell: 'Fifty pounds to whoever catches that dog!'

As the ribbon disappeared into a forest of legs, he upped the reward: 'A hundred pounds! Two hundred! Somebody *STOP THAT DOG!*'

Two hundred pounds?

People craned their necks to catch a glimpse of the dog he was talking about. Suddenly there were hands reaching down for Sam from every side.

Wham! A man in a top hat stamped one boot down on the golden lead but Sam strained forward and the lead snapped.

Whoosh! A girl in a blue dress made a grab for him, but at the last minute Sam darted between her hands.

Yuugghh! An old woman hooked her umbrella handle through Sam's collar, but the collar broke.

Somebody yanked the little dog's tail. Somebody else trod on his foot. Sam growled and dodged and wriggled. If only he could get away from the crowd . . .

Suddenly, through the forest of legs, he met a pair of eyes at exactly the same level as his own. They belonged to the scruffiest dog he'd ever seen.

This way! the dog barked. *Follow me – and run!*

And Sam did.

The next ten minutes were the most astonishing ones of his life. He raced round corners and scampered down alleys. He belted up flights of steps, through yards, and across gardens. He wriggled under hedges, jumped over fences, and splashed through puddles. Somewhere along the way he lost his ribbon.

'Stop that dog!' Fred cried, leading the chase.

'Which dog?' a man asked in bewilderment as first one dog and then another rocketed between his legs.

'The Emperor's dog!' the shout came back. '*After him!*'

On and on Sam raced, until his sides hurt and his mouth felt as if it was on fire. Suddenly: *This way!* the other dog barked, and led him through some bushes into the opening of an enormous pipe that ran beneath the city streets. It didn't smell much like the palace.

At the other end of the pipe was a river. *Can you swim?* the other dog barked. *Never mind – just do what I do! Follow me!*

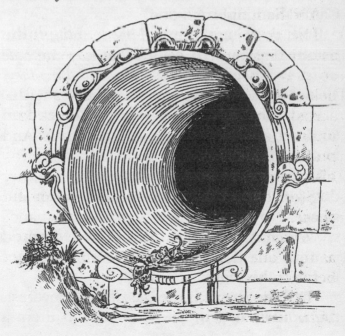

Somehow, Sam did.

When the two dogs had scrambled on to the bank a quarter of a mile downstream, the scruffy dog rolled in the dust. Sam looked around for the velvet towel, but there didn't seem to be one.

He rolled in the dust too.

He was still rolling when the shouting started again, very close.

'There he is!' Fred shouted. 'Catch him! Catch the Emperor's dog!'

Both dogs jumped up. *Time to split up,* the scruffy dog barked. *You go that way and hide under the bridge. I'll go this way and draw them off. See you in a while.* He was off like a flash.

Under the bridge it was cool and quiet. Sam lay down and rested his nose on his paws. And because he was very tired, he fell asleep.

Meanwhile . . . the crowd chasing the other dog got bigger and bigger, and closer and closer. No matter which way he ran, hands were waiting to grab him. Two hundred pounds is a lot of money. Everyone wanted to catch the Emperor's dog.

The little dog was the fittest, the cleverest, the boldest dog in the city. He led them a fine dance, and he enjoyed every minute. All the same, in the end he nipped round a corner and there was Fred!

'Ha! Got you, your dogginess!' Fred pounced in triumph.

Your who?

'Come on!' He tucked the squirming animal firmly under one arm. 'We're going home.'

When Sam woke up, the strip of sky beyond the bridge was the colour of pewter. He sat up and began to think about dinner. For the first time in months, he felt hungry. He whined – a small, sad noise he wouldn't have made if he'd thought anyone could hear him.

'Scruff?' said a voice.

An avalanche of dirt and stones slid down the bank, followed by a girl, thin and ragged, scratched and grubby.

'Scruff?' Anna said again, peering into the gloom. 'Is that you?'

No, of course it's not. Do I look like a Scruff? Sam was too tired to run. He stayed on, hoping she wouldn't see him.

She took one step into the gloom. She took two steps. And then . . .

'*Scruff!*' she cried joyfully. 'I've been looking *everywhere*. Come here, you bad dog you!' She scooped him into her arms.

Help! I'm being dog-napped!

'It's no use barking.' She gave him a fond hug. 'I'm taking you home.'

Chapter Five

Fred got the telling-off to end all telling-offs, with half the palace listening. 'Go!' Lord Hawk finally thundered. 'Back to the garden, with the slugs and the toads and the vipers, where you belong.'

'Oh,' said Fred, crestfallen. 'There aren't any vipers, as a matter . . .' He caught Lord Hawk's eye. 'Right. Sorry. Shall I take the trousers back to Carl first?'

Lord Hawk shuddered. 'Burn them. They smell of . . . of agriculture. So do you. Give me the gruckle hound and be gone!'

Fred hesitated. 'You sure you want him, my lord? He's – well, he's not *clean*, exactly.' The understatement of the century.

'I have eyes,' said the Emperor's advisor, superbly scornful. 'For the last time, hand over the dog and get out!'

Fred shrugged, and obeyed.

'Ughmmn!' said Lord Hawk faintly, getting a noseful of smells straight from the city sewers. 'Whaaaghgrmrugh?'

'He's trod in something,' said a poker-faced footman, edging away. 'Poor blighter.'

'Rolled in it, more like,' said another. 'He don't half pong, my lord.'

'He could do with a bath,' said a third, unwisely.

'See to it,' Lord Hawk said, thrusting the dog at him. 'One bath. Two baths. As many baths as it takes. Tell Carl to do it – it's all his fault for catching a cold. Don't bring the dog back until he looks and smells as the Emperor's gruckle hound should.'

'Yughughrm, my lord,' gasped the footman.

'Keep still,' Anna told Sam sternly as she rubbed hard, pink soap into his coat. 'I know you hate it, but you haven't had a bath for months.'

What do you mean? I had one this morning.

'I don't know what you've been up to, but you're starting to smell really *doggy*.'

I beg your pardon?!

The soap was the most horrible thing Sam had ever smelt. The water from the tap was so cold it hurt. After the first yelp, however, he suffered in silence, because that's what you do if you're an Emperor's dog.

'That's better!' she said at last, rubbing him dry. 'And you've been so good. No growling, no running away. You haven't even tried to bite me! Let's go and find you some dinner.'

Good! I'm in the mood for Beef Wellington, and perhaps a small portion of truffles. Have you got that?

She gave him a hug and carried him inside.

'Ohbigod!' Carl turned his head away as he lifted Scruff into a steaming silver-plated bath-tub.

Hey! What do you think I am? A blooming lobster?

'Gib be the rosewater!' Carl emptied in half a bottle of perfume, and reached for a sponge.

I don't need a bath. I had one last year.

'How cad you get so dirty in wud day?' Carl demanded, up to his elbows in bubbles. He emptied the rest of the rosewater into the tub, and reached for a scrubbing brush.

Scruff stopped yelping and growled. *Don't even think about it, mate.*

Ten seconds later. 'Ow!' Carl dropped the scrubbing brush into the bath-tub. 'Hey!

Ouch! Cub back here! You've got to be dried, ad cobed, ad have a dew ribbud for the codcert, ad – I said *Cub back!*'

Catch me!

Off the little dog raced, leaving a trail of puddles all the way up the marble hall.

Dinner? Sam asked himself. *What dinner?*

Where was his dinner-plate? Where was his Beef Wellington, with a side serving of salad?

All he could see was a heap of scraps in a broken saucer. He wasn't meant to eat that, was he?

'Mmmhm . . .' Anna's eyes narrowed. 'Not hungry tonight? Been sticking our nose in Mr Gruber's dustbin, have we?'

I beg your pardon?

'Been stealing the fish-heads Auntie Hannah puts out for her cat?'

Oh, please . . .

'Or have we run off with another string of sausages? Don't look all innocent: you've got no secrets from me.'

She put the saucer up on the table. 'That's it. You're not getting anything else tonight, so it's no good whining later.'

I never whine.

Her voice changed. 'You'll just have to make do with your BONE!'

Sam sat down in the middle of the floor and looked at her.

'I said, you'll just have to make do with your BONE!'

Mad, quite mad. A pity. Sam sighed and lay down.

Anna flung herself down beside him. 'I said BONE, Scruff, BONE. Go and get it, then,' she urged anxiously. 'I wasn't really cross, you know. I wouldn't want you any different. Bone! Bone! BO-O-O-NE! Are you sick or something? It's under the chair where you left it. Look!' She stood up, brandishing what looked like an elephant's shinbone. 'Here it is, your very own lovely bone!'

Lovely? A bone another dog had been chewing for the past six months? No – Sam advanced his nose to within an inch of the bone and winced – better make that the past year.

You're asking me to chew a second-hand bone?

He wasn't that hungry, and he didn't think he ever would be.

Scruff stared at the jewelled dinner-plate with its tiny helping of minced liver in a light sherry sauce, with a side serving of cucumber.

That's dinner? Is this some kind of joke?

Where was his saucer? Where was the other half of the pork pie Anna had saved from her breakfast, and the mutton fat Auntie Hannah had brought over on Sunday? Where was his bone?

He turned away from the plate with an angry growl.

They can't ask me to eat muck like this. It's horrible.

'Dot hugry?' Carl blew his nose. 'Go without, thed. It'll do you good. You eat too buch edyway. Cub od. It's quarter to seved: tibe for the codcert.'

Thanks for the warning, mate. Now, where do I hide?

As the church clock struck, Anna opened the door to the stairs, and jiggled the door-handle. 'Upstairs,' she commanded. 'It's music practice!'

Sam sat up and put his head on one side.

Anna looked back at him in surprise. 'Off

63

you go! I'm going to play my violin. You know how you feel about it. Go on upstairs and hide under the bed where you can't hear.'

Sam gave an encouraging bark. *Hide? You've got me wrong. I love music.*

She shut the door again. 'Stay if you want, but don't say I didn't warn you. And if you *dare* howl, or bark, or so much as whine, you're finished, do you hear?'

Relax, I'm not that sort of dog.

She stood on a chair to reach her violin case down from the shelf. When she opened the case and put the violin to her chin, he sat to attention and waited eagerly for her to raise the bow.

The news spread like wildfire all through the palace. By half-past seven even Fred, dusting roses in the courtyard, had heard it: the concert had had to be cancelled. The last of the gruckle hounds was sick.

'What do you mean, sick? What's wrong with him?' He dropped the feather duster and ran after the footman who had brought the news.

'No one knows,' the footman called over

his shoulder. 'It's serious, though. You should have heard him howl when they started playing . . . there's never been anything like it. They've sent for old Henderson.'

'Wow!' said Fred slowly. Even he knew that you had to be very rich and important to be one of Doctor Henderson's patients.

The Emperor had never sent for his personal physician in the night before. The doctor rushed to the palace in his silk pyjamas, ready to save the Emperor's life.

'Have no fear, I am here!' he cried, sweeping into the concert hall. 'Where is my patient?'

'There!' Lord Hawk pointed at Scruff, who was trying to scratch off his purple ribbon.

'*That* is the patient?' Doctor Henderson looked at Lord Hawk. 'You sent for me to treat a *dog*?'

Scruff cocked his head. *He's slow, but he gets there.*

'To treat the Emperor's dog?' Lord Hawk raised his eyebrows. 'To treat the last of the gruckle hounds? Naturally.'

Doctor Henderson swallowed. 'Naturally. Well, I will see what I can do.'

'Naturally,' said the Emperor.

Doctor Henderson lifted one of Scruff's front paws and consulted his watch.

The dog growled. *Do you mind?*

'Dear me,' the doctor said, 'this dog is *very* sick.' He released the paw. 'Say *Ah!*' he told the dog sternly.

Who does he think he is, giving me orders? Scruff flattened his ears and barked.

Doctor Henderson shook his head and looked grave. 'Thank heavens you called me when you did. Another hour – another ten minutes even . . .' He shook his head again.

'It might have been too late. As it is, a small injection will do the trick. Hold the patient!' he ordered Lord Hawk.

'Hold the patient!' Lord Hawk ordered Carl smartly.

We'll see about that!

'You see?' the Emperor said breathlessly a moment later, from the top of a bench. 'My gruckle hound is sick. He acts as if we were gruckles. You must do something to save him.'

Doctor Henderson had had enough. 'He's too sick for me, your highness. I suggest you consult Doctor—' He named his greatest rival, and said goodnight.

Off the limousine raced, taking the doctor home. It returned first with his great rival and then with one after another of the best doctors in the city.

It was no good.

The Emperor's gruckle hound was sick, and not a doctor could be found to cure him.

'There!' Anna laid down her bow. 'That wasn't so bad, was it?' She turned round from the music stand and blinked. 'Scruff? Scruff, where are you?'

Sam emerged cautiously from under the sofa.

He hadn't realised a violin could sound like that.

He hadn't realised *anything* could sound like that. Except maybe a dying vacuum cleaner.

'And you didn't howl once! Good dog!' Anna said fondly, throwing both arms around him and hugging him tight.

I couldn't howl. I was in shock.

'Maybe he'll turn out musical after all,' Gregory said, much amused when she told him. 'After all, the Emperor's dog loves Beethoven, so Gruber was telling me.'

Beethoven? Please . . . I'm a Mozart dog.

Gregory yawned and strolled over to the shelf in the corner. 'But I doubt if the Emperor's dog has as many fleas as this one.' He handed her a rusty tin. 'Dust him down with flea powder, Anna. Gruber was scratching all evening, and he swears it's because he stroked Scruff last week.'

Anna took the tin of powder. 'All right, but it's silly,' she said huffily. 'Scruff *doesn't* have fleas. Do you, my dearest?' she said fondly, opening the tin.

Fleas? Sam put his head on one side. *What are those when they're at home?*

Whoof! The room disappeared behind a cloud of flea powder.

'I said dust him down,' Gregory gasped, wiping his eyes, 'not smother him.'

'Better safe than sorry,' Anna said firmly. 'Mr Gruber's never going to get the chance to say you've got fleas again, Scruff.' She upended the tin once more.

Because I'll be dead? wondered Sam in the split second before he started sneezing.

The clock struck midnight as Carl put Scruff out into the courtyard.

At last! Thought I was going to burst for a minute.

Fred was there, arranging pebbles in patterns under the roses. Last month they'd been laid out like a chequer-board. This month it was going to be circles. Then stripes, then waves, then zig-zags, then polka dots. Than a chequer board again.

Talk about pointless.

With a sigh, he reached into his pocket for a bar of chocolate.

'Don't you whine at me,' he told Scruff as he peeled off the wrapper. 'Almost got me sacked, you did. Won't catch me playing with you again in a hurry.'

Let me out of here! Scruff sat down at the gate and began to howl.

'Hey, I didn't mean it, your dogginess,' Fred said, relenting. 'What's wrong, eh? You don't look sick to me, just sad.' He put the chocolate bar down on the head of a small stone angel, and rubbed the little dog's chest.

Scruff stopped howling and sniffed. *Chocolate?*

He looked almost as if he wanted something . . . Fred picked up the chocolate bar and took a bite.

Scruff raised his two front paws in the air and gave a long, complicated whine.

Anyone would think he was begging, Fred thought, with a grin. As if the Emperor's dog had to beg for anything!

What does a dog have to do round here to get a bite to eat? Turn somersaults? Dance a polka?

Well, if begging didn't work there were other ways.

'Hey!' Fred gasped. 'Give that bar back! That

was my supper, that was!'

And very nice too. Scruff wagged his tail and licked the boy's hand. *No hard feelings?*

Fred stared at the damp patch on his wrist in disbelief. 'What's going on? You've never done that before! What's got into you?'

I want to go home. Scruff scratched urgently at the courtyard gate.

'I can't let you out,' Fred said, exasperated. 'The only person who's got a key is the sentry. But I will find your ball, the first chance I get, all right?'

Bull? Do I look as if I'm in the mood for playing?

'You're bad,' Carl commented from the palace door. 'Stark, starig, bokkers. What you goig to be talkig to dext, wurbs? Brig hib over here, would you? I'b goig to bed. Thacks.'

He carried the little dog wriggling and squirming into the palace.

'Could be the full moon,' Gregory said, sitting down on the top stair. 'That can make dogs restless.'

I'm not asking you, I'm telling you – no, I am positively commanding you to open this door.

'He's never been like this.' Anna sat on the

71

bottom stair, wearing one of her father's old shirts as a nightdress, held together with patches. She'd tied the front bits of her hair up in rags, to see if that would make it curl. The bits at the back hung straight, as always.

'He won't come up on my bed.'

Gruckle hounds don't. I told you.

'He won't come when I call.'

I refuse to answer to a name like Scruff.

'He must be sick. Maybe I gave him too much flea powder?' She spoke in the gruff voice she used when she was worried.

The less said about that the better. I'm considering legal action.

'For heaven's sake!' Gregory gave her an affectionate prod in the back with one toe. 'Does a sick dog march up and down, barking, as if he was in a parade? I don't know what's wrong with him, but he's not sick. Maybe he needs to pop outside.'

Yes! Yes! Open the door!

Anna looked up in alarm. 'You mustn't let him out! What if he doesn't come back?'

'All right.' Her father sighed. 'Find me his collar and the rope you use as a lead, and I'll take him for a walk. That'll settle him down, you'll see. And then maybe a man can get a wink of sleep.'

Scruff lay on the marble floor outside the Emperor's room. He missed Anna.

The floor was cold and hard. There'd been a cushion once, but he'd chewed it up hours ago, and scattered the stuffing up and down the hall.

He missed Anna a lot.

He'd stuck his nose into the kennel and nothing on earth was going to make him go inside. It smelt of the dark, and of being shut in. He'd tried to find a way out of the palace, but no matter which way he went down the corridor, he arrived at a door too heavy to nose open.

He missed Anna *terribly*.

He even missed Tom and Arnold. He could do with a bit of all-for-one-and-one-for-all at the moment. He pressed his nose to the crack beneath the nearest door and whined.

Nobody came.

Perhaps he could dig an escape tunnel through the marble floor?

There was only one way to find out.

Half an hour later, the Emperor took the pillow off his head. He put on his brocade dressing-gown and his fur-lined slippers, and opened the door.

At last!

Scruff tore past him into the room, jumped up on the bed, turned round three times and lay down. Within moments he was asleep.

For a whole minute, the Emperor was too stunned to say anything. Then he cleared his throat. 'This is not correct,' he said firmly, holding the door open. 'Kindly leave at once.'

Scruff started to snore.

The back streets at night were another world to a dog used to the palace.

The noises were different. No tinkling fountain – instead the creak of an inn sign swinging in the wind, the bang of a distant door, and furtive scuffling sounds from somewhere too close for comfort.

Sam sniffed the air. It smelt different too. He had a hunch that they didn't grow roses in this part of town. Instead they seemed to grow orange peel, empty beer cans, old newspapers, and – Sam nosed the remains of a hamburger in the gutter – revolting greasy things that reeked of onions.

'Go ahead,' said Gregory with a yawn. 'I don't care. It's your stomach, not mine. Eat it if you want to. You've had worse.'

Worse? You mean there are worse *things to eat than this?*

A cat slipped out of the shadows. *Fair shares, remember?* It slapped one hefty paw down on the slab of meat. *Arnold's asleep, so we'll make it a two way split, OK?*

I beg your pardon? Have we met? Who's Arnold?

The cat didn't reply at once, but when exactly half the hamburger was gone, it licked its whiskers. *Still the comedian, I see. The rest's yours. Oh, and there's half a sausage behind Gruber's dustbin. I left it for you. All for one and one for all. See you.* The cat swarmed up a wall, flicked its tail, and vanished.

'Come on!' Gregory gave the string a tug. 'I can't stand here all night. I'm tired. Quick march!'

At last, there was something a dog *could* understand! Nose high, tail erect, and head spinning, the Emperor's gruckle hound quick-marched into the night.

Chapter Six

Hollow-eyed from lack of sleep and stiff from a night on the floor, the Emperor rose and headed straight for the library. There were seventeen thousand, three hundred and fifty-six books there, and it seemed a fair bet that one of the books had something useful to say about looking after a sick gruckle hound.

The trouble was, none of them did.

There wasn't a single word about the gruckle hound. Or the gruckle.

Lord Hawk smothered a yawn. 'Never mind, your highness. If the hound dies, the Guild can give you a new mascot.'

'Dies?' the Emperor said, alarmed. 'You think he might *die*, Hawk?'

'Possibly. But it doesn't matter.'

It struck the Emperor in a flash that what he wanted most in the world was to hit his

advisor over the head with the large globe that sat on the library table. 'What do you mean "it doesn't matter"?'

'There are other exotic beasts. The slimy Mongolian swamp lizard, for example. I happen to know that the Guild is seeking homes for several fine specimens. Leave it to me, and I'll have one delivered within the hour.'

'I don't want a swamp lizard,' the Emperor cried. 'I want my gruckle hound, the way he used to be.' He took a deep breath and uncurled his fingers from the base of the globe. 'You *must* remember your gruckle-hunting days, Hawk! Surely there's something that would help? Special food? A tonic? A psychiatrist? Think, Hawk, think!'

Something about the way the Emperor glanced at the globe as he spoke made Lord Hawk think both hard and fast. 'There is a boy, your highness,' he said at last, 'the one who brought the gruckle hound in on the night of your birthday. He works in the garden. He claims to have learned about gruckle hounds at his grandmother's knee. I *could* have him sent for.'

'At once!' the Emperor cried. 'Send for the boy and the gruckle hound at once!'

Out in the courtyard, Carl and Fred perched on the edge of the fountain, watching Scruff try to dig up the paving stones by the gate to the street.

'I don't know what's got into him,' Carl said for the seventh time.

'*I* don't know what's got into him,' Fred replied frowning.

'You know how he loves his morning bath? Well, all of a sudden, he doesn't. Took three of us to get him in the tub this morning. And the noise! Next thing, he goes and turns up his nose at his favourite breakfast.'

'Weird.' Fred shook his head, baffled. 'Dogs don't *do* that. If they like something, they like it. They don't change their mind the way people do.'

'This one does,' Carl pointed out. 'He's changed his mind about food, about baths and concerts, all since yesterday. And he's forgotten stuff too: do you know what he did just now? Tried to get out here through the door to the linen cupboard! I had to show him the way to his own garden!'

Fred pursed his lips in a soundless whistle. 'Spooky!'

'It's like he's never been in the palace before.'

'Like a different dog.'

'Yeah,' said Carl. 'That's it exactly. Ever since you took him out yesterday, he's like a different dog.'

A strange sensation hit Fred, like being brained with a cricket bat. He staggered and clutched at his forehead.

'Oh no!' he whispered as the truth dawned in a blinding flash. 'That's what he *is*! He's a different dog! I brought back the wrong one!'

'You!' said a voice from the doorway.

Carl and Fred jumped apart as if a cannonball had landed between them.

'Yes, you,' Lord Hawk gave Fred an earth-scorching glare. 'Wipe the mud off your boots, take the caterpillar out of your hair, collect the gruckle hound, and follow me. The Emperor wants you.'

Sam sat in the tiny yard behind Anna's house, waiting. In his experience, if you waited long

80

enough, sooner or later someone fed you. Or bathed you. Or took you out to march in a parade. Or something.

He yawned and laid his nose on his paws. If he shut his eyes it was just like being back home in his kennel.

Perhaps he *was* back home in his kennel? Perhaps he'd had a horrible dream brought on by eating too much minced liver? He didn't feel as if he'd eaten too much – just the opposite – but you couldn't tell with dreams.

He opened one eye cautiously, and shut it again, fast.

If it was a dream, he was still having it. And it was more like a nightmare. Why else should he suddenly find himself eyeball to eyeball with the fattest bird he had ever seen? He opened the eye again, long enough to see that the battered shape beyond the bird was the cat from the night before.

By day, it looked even worse.

Sam sat up straight and tried to look like a dog you tangled with at your peril.

You're right, the bird said. *It isn't Scruff.*

Obviously. Scruff would have got out through the gap behind the dustbin. The cat flicked his tail. *Wonder what's happened to him? I've got plans for today. We need him.* He looked at Sam thoughtfully. *Or someone like him.*

There's no one like Scruff, the pigeon objected.

Granted. He doesn't have to be a genius, though. A dog with half a brain will do. Let's try. The cat gave a blood-curdling growl. *Hey, you! Want to stay here the rest of your life?*

The cat interrupted before Sam was halfway through his answer.

We'll get you out, then. All you have to do is one small favour in return.

Anything, Sam barked eagerly, *anything at all!*

Carl slid into the seat next to Fred at supper. 'Thought you'd be in the dungeons by now. What happ—'

'Don't ask.' Fred's normally cheerful face had a glazed look – the look of someone who's spent eight hours on the trot trying to explain why a perfectly behaved gruckle hound who knows the palace like the back of its paw should suddenly behave as if it had never been there before in its life. 'I want to forget.' He scratched the back of his neck and gave a heavy sigh.

Carl ate half a sandwich in sympathetic silence. 'Were you right, though? *Is* it a different—'

'Oh yes.' Fred stared broodingly into space as he chewed a crust. 'It bit the German ambassador. I had to tell the Emperor it was because there was gruckle oil in his aftershave.'

'What?' Carl said, startled.

'It was all I could think of. Only, the ambassador's got a beard like a beaver. So then I had to say I meant his before-shave. The Emperor asked him about it through the interpreter.' Fred chewed on bleakly.

'And?'

'The ambassador got the idea the Emperor wanted him to shave his beard off. He didn't seem to like that.' Fred pushed aside his plate. 'But I missed the next bit because the dog was sick over Hawk-Eye's boots. It wasn't my fault,' Fred cried with feeling, 'if he nicked food off people's plates at lunch and it disagreed with him. I couldn't do anything about it. And now Hawk-Eye says if I make one more mistake he'll have me thrown out into the street. It's not fair.'

Carl scratched his right shoulder, then his left. He absentmindedly scratched the right one again. 'You're in a bit of a fix, aren't you? If they find out there's another dog the spitting image of him, right here in the city, they'll know for sure he's not the last of the gruckle hounds. Do I have a rash? I'm all itchy.'

'Oh, I forgot.' Fred gave a hollow laugh. 'You haven't got a rash. I've come over itchy too, and so have a lot of other people. Anyone who's been near the dog, if you want to know. Tomorrow the whole blooming court'll be scratching.'

Carl looked at him, round-eyed. 'You mean . . . ?'

'Got it in one.' Fred stood up. 'I need to get those dogs swapped back again quick smart, before the Court finds out that . . .' he swallowed and then continued steadily, 'that I've given them fleas.'

A long way away from the palace, Sam crouched in a dark, smelly tunnel. In the light of recent events, he was glad to be there.

It could have been worse, far worse.

Wonderful! The cat spoke sourly from the gloom. *A real triumph. Remind me to ask you to be lookout again, will you? Next time I want to get eaten alive by a bulldog, and wind up in the sewer.*

Next time I fancy having my tailfeathers blown off by a maniac with a shotgun. Comrade, a voice to his right added sternly.

It came as a surprise to Sam that pigeons were so sarcastic.

You were meant to be on our side – or didn't I mention that? The cat growled. *For future reference, when I am being chased by an angry crowd shouting Stop thief! it doesn't help if you jump out from behind a dustbin and knock me flat. Right?*

I didn't know it was you they were chasing, Sam said with spirit. *You told me you'd gone to see a man about a cat. Nothing about stopping off to rob a fish shop. I'd never have helped if I'd known you were doing something illegal.*

You didn't help.

That's the point, said Arnold.

Has it occurred to you, comrade, that if it hadn't been for Arnold and me here, you would now be no more than a nasty mess on the pavement outside the fish shop? Which would be sad for Anna.

And for us, Arnold added severely.

And for us, the cat was stunned to hear himself say. *Heaven knows why, but I'd miss you. So be more careful next time.*

Next time? Sam's heart leapt, but he sat like a statue, every muscle at attention. *When? Now? Are we going to try again this evening?*

Don't see why not, the cat said tolerantly, *Comrade.*

Chapter Seven

By morning even Fred was ready to admit that the gruckle hound problem was an uncommonly difficult nut to crack. He was going to get precious little chance to think about it, too, to judge by the list of jobs lined up for him.

'It's stupid, this is,' he muttered as he set to work picking cobwebs off the roses. 'Who minds a few cobwebs? They're *nice*, cobwebs are. They belong here. Look at this one! It's . . . it's . . . it's a miracle, that's what it is. And I've got to spoil it! Sorry, mate,' he said sadly as a spider scuttled for cover. 'Head gardener's orders.'

What if he came clean about bringing back the wrong dog?

Easy. He'd get fired. 'But the way things are going he'll do that anyway,' he told a passing beetle. 'One little slip-up, that's all it'll take! One!' The beetle had a sympathetic face so he went on. 'What's so great about this job anyway? Two years I've been here, and all they ever let me do is pull stuff up! That's not my idea of gardening.'

The door from the palace swung open. 'You!' snapped a familiar voice. 'Come here! Heaven knows why, but the Emperor requires your presence. And remember, boy—' the beetle scuttled for cover under a fallen rose leaf, 'remember that your next mistake will be your last.'

'Yes my lord, sorry my lord.' Fred scrambled to his feet.

The Emperor was pacing restlessly up and down the drawing-room. He'd had a terrible night. At half-past two he'd tried to lure the dog off the bed by laying a trail of chocolates across the floor. It had eaten the chocolates, which was good, then jumped back on to the bed, which wasn't.

At four o'clock it had been unwell all over the sheets.

'he gruckle hound is still sick,' he told

Fred, looking pale and tense. 'I must find out what's wrong. And you're the only person who can help.'

Lord Hawk quivered all over. 'The boy had his chance yesterday, your highness. He failed. That is only to be expected: he is, when all is said and done, a nincompoop. I understand the swamp lizard is still available, incidentally. Shall I inform the society that you are interested?'

'No!' The Emperor's eyes flashed. 'I don't want a swamp lizard! I never have wanted a swamp lizard! I never will want a swamp lizard. I want my gruckle hound, and I want him happy. And since nobody here seems to be the slightest use – including you, Hawk – I am going to send for an expert.'

'The kennel master?' Lord Hawk sniffed.

'Not the kennel master.' Fred jumped as the Emperor placed a hand on his shoulder. 'I am going to send for the woman who taught this boy all he knows about gruckle hounds: his grandmother!'

'No!' Fred cried in dismay. 'You can't do that! She's . . . she's too old to travel!'

'I'll send a car,' the Emperor replied, 'and

Doctor Henderson to look after her. Where does she live?'

'Miles and miles away. And she'd be no use. She . . . she forgets things. And she can't talk too well because she lost her teeth in a . . . a hunting accident! And she's deaf,' Fred cried wildly, casting about for a cast-iron excuse. 'I mean dead! Yes, that's it: she died last summer. I knew there was something,' he finished more calmly.

The Emperor's face fell. 'Dead?'

'Why didn't you say so at once, fool,' snapped Lord Hawk, 'instead of wittering on about her forgetting things? Of course she forgets things if she's dead! It's under-standable. Stop wasting the Emperor's valuable time.'

'Sshh!' The Emperor flung up a hand. 'Be quiet, Hawk. I've got the answer! *Gruckles!*'

Lord Hawk and Fred stared at him, baffled.

'Don't you understand? We'll send for some gruckles!'

Fred made the sort of noise people make when they've been kicked in the stomach.

'What surer way to stop a gruckle hound

pining than a gruckle hunt?' the Emperor went on in triumph. 'It's perfect, Hawk. I'm surprised you didn't think of it yourself – you being so clever and all.'

It was too much. In the past fifteen minutes Lord Hawk had been shouted at and shushed more than he had in his whole life. And now the Emperor – who had always been putty in his hands – appeared by some fluke to have solved the gruckle hound problem before Lord Hawk could himself!

It was more than too much. It was the last straw.

'As a matter of fact,' Lord Hawk said furiously, 'I did think of it myself. This morning. At breakfast. And I took the liberty of sending for the gruckles there and then. If you will excuse me, I must go and see if the messenger has reported back.'

'Ooof???!?' Fred said. '*Oooofff?*'

'Keep him with you every minute,' Gregory warned as he fastened his pack. 'I don't want another scene like last night, with half the city on the doorstep, complaining about your wretched dog.'

Sam slunk prudently under the sofa.

'*Our* wretched dog,' Anna reminded him. 'He's as much yours as mine.'

'Not any more,' her father said with feeling. 'Stealing a salmon, of all things! The most expensive fish you can buy! And two pounds of fillet steak, at £6.50 a pound! That's a whole day's wages gone, Anna. Then he has the gall to come marching back as if he was proud of himself. You'd think he'd have more sense.'

'It was clever, though.' Anna's foot stretched under the sofa and scratched Sam comfortingly on his chest. 'How many dogs would think of smuggling themselves into the best food store in the city by hiding inside someone's shopping basket? Or know the best things to run off with? He's never *seen* a salmon before, let alone tasted one. And the only meat he gets is scraps from Aunt Hannah. So he really was clever, wasn't he? Very bad too, of course,' she added as she caught her father's eye. 'And he's never going to do anything like that again, ever.'

That's right, thought Sam. *Never.*

Unless I'm helping a friend, or keeping a promise,

I will absolutely definitely almost never steal anything again.

'He'd better not,' Gregory said grimly as he hoisted his pack onto his shoulder. 'Another thing: if I see so much as a whisker of that cat, or one feather of that dratted pigeon when I come home, I won't be responsible for my actions.'

After the door had slammed, the cat strolled out from behind the kitchen dresser. Seconds later there was a loud plop as a well fed pigeon landed on the window-sill.

'Did you hear that?' Anna asked sternly. 'All of you? You'd better behave today, or else! And as for you, Scruff—'

Her toes reached under the sofa and scratched just the best place on Sam's chest. Sam meant to twitch his tail, but somehow it wagged instead.

He looked at it in surprise.

'As for you, you wicked dog, I'm not going to let you out of my sight.'

As Sam looked up at her, it happened again: his tail wagged again, quite of its own accord. *Would you care to lay a small wager?* he wondered.

'Gruckles?' The messenger blinked. Privately he thought Lord Hawk was losing his marbles, but it didn't do to say so. 'You want six fully-grown gruckles? Here? By tomorrow? Where do I get them, my lord?' And what the flipping heck *are* they, he felt like adding.

'That's up to you,' Lord Hawk snapped. 'Take the plane, take a car, take a team of motor-bikes if you need to, but go now, and don't come back without them!'

'You haven't got a picture or anything?' The messenger looked at him pleadingly. 'I mean, to tell the truth, my lord, I'm a bit rusty on gruckles. It's a while since I saw one. In the flesh, that is. Could you give me a bit of a clue, like?'

Lord Hawk was not prepared to give him a clue. He said so, at full volume for several minutes. 'Get out of here at once,' he finished furiously, 'and let me have those gruckles first thing tomorrow!'

The messenger sprang to attention. 'No problem, my lord. I'll get the plane out right away.'

The moment Fred got his breath back, he did the sensible thing: told the Emperor that he couldn't have a gruckle-hunt because gruckles were extinct.

'No, they're not,' the Emperor said confidently.

'Honestly, your highness, they are. My gran wrote and told me. The last gruckle was run over by a . . . steam-roller outside her house. She saw the whole thing.'

'But you said your grandmother was dead.'

The Emperor didn't sound suspicious so much as puzzled.

'She is! The shock killed her. She wrote to tell me what had happened, posted the letter, and . . .' Fred's imagination gave up, so he shook his head sadly, and looked at his feet.

'I thought you said she died in a hunting accident?' On a scale of one to ten, the Emperor looked as if he'd have scored in the high nines for bafflement. Fred was beginning to feel the same himself. 'Do you mean they hunt gruckles on *steam-rollers*?'

There seemed to be only one answer to that. 'Yes,' Fred said baldly. Before the Emperor had a chance to ask for details, he went on: 'So it's no good Lord Hawk looking for gruckles, your highness. There aren't any left.'

'Nonsense!' the Emperor said robustly. 'Your grandmother died last summer, and Lord Hawk told me only yesterday that he saw two gruckles last month when he was walking in the Alps. Rare they may be, but certainly *not* extinct. And however rare they are, Hawk will find them. The animal he cannot find does not exist.'

Too true, Fred thought, trying not to panic.

'But . . . but if you start hunting rare animals, you make them extinct,' he cried. 'Those six gruckles may be the last on the whole planet! You can't sacrifice them to cheer up one gruckle hound!'

That aspect of the situation hadn't occurred to the Emperor. His face clouded over. 'I can't? What about sacrificing three gruckles? Or two?' He looked pleadingly at Fred. 'Oh, couldn't I even let him hunt one?'

'No,' Fred said sternly. 'It would be wrong. A gruckle has a right to live too. It may have big teeth—'

'Enormous teeth,' the Emperor reminded him. 'And a deadly gruckle horn.'

'Enormous teeth, and a deadly horn, but—'

'And cruel claws. Don't forget those.'

'Look,' Fred cried, beginning to get worked up, 'gruckles may have teeth and horns and claws and all that, but they're not so bad. They have a very nice home life, for one thing, and they . . they *cry* when they're frightened. They just want to be left alone. They don't ask anyone to come thundering after them baying for blood. If you ask me, people like Lord Hawk deserve everything they get.'

The words were like music to the Emperor's ears. 'Yes!' he cried, springing to his feet. 'You're right!' He seized Fred by the shoulders with a view to kissing him on both cheeks, when a less agreeable thought struck him. 'But what am I going to do about my gruckle hound? If there's no gruckle hunt, how on earth can we stop the poor creature pining?'

'There's lots of ways,' said Fred passionately. 'Stop thinking gruckle hound, and start thinking dog, your highness. Don't think gruckles, think . . . think strokes!'

'Strokes!' The Emperor blinked.

'Yes!' Fred cried. 'Think pats! Think scratch-on-the-head. Think tickle-on-the-tummy and rub-on-the-chest. Get him to fetch a stick for you. Throw him a ball . . .'

Fred stopped in mid flow as if someone had turned off the tap.

The ball! That was how the whole crisis began. Even if the Emperor called off the gruckle hunt, that still left Fred with a big problem.

Two problems, rather: Sam and his twin brother, currently moping beneath the throne, nose on paws, too fed-up even to bark.

How on earth could he unsnarl the mix-up before the whole world woke up to what had happened?

The Emperor had pulled out a small leather-bound diary and a gold fountain pen. 'Strokes,' he muttered, frowning. 'Scratches, and – what was the other thing? Pats?' He looked up, pen poised. 'Do I need special gloves? Are you sure? What about the risk of infection? Well, if you say so . . . Is there anything else I should try that dogs like?'

Then it happened: a brainwave of such dazzling brilliance it took Fred's breath away.

'A walk!' he whispered.

Why hadn't he thought of it before? It was so simple! Take the wrong dog for a walk, slip into town, track down Sam, swap the dogs back, and bring Sam home again before any other disasters happened. With a bit of luck – well overdue in Fred's opinion – once Sam was back, behaving as perfectly as he always did, the Emperor would calm down, and there'd be no more nonsense about gruckle hunts or fetching people's grandmothers. All he had to do was persuade the Emperor to let him take the dog out.

Fred fixed his eyes hypnotically on the Emperor's face and talked for five minutes non-stop.

'Take him for a walk? *On foot?*' the Emperor asked in alarm. 'Wouldn't a ride in my car do instead? He likes that.' So did the Emperor, especially when Sam stuck his head out through the window and shut his eyes.

It was no time for Fred to mince words. 'A ride's no good at all, your highness. I promise, he'll enjoy a walk a lot more. And I'll take him now, if you like. Here, boy!'

Fred clicked his fingers. Scruff looked up, recognised Fred from the day before, and came to have his head scratched.

'Wait!' The Emperor knew he ought to be pleased to see his gruckle hound showing an interest in life, but he wasn't. He wished he'd thought of clicking his fingers himself. 'You really think a walk will be good for him?'

Fred nodded. 'I'm sure of it,' he said, itching to be gone.

The Emperor squared his shoulders. 'Then a walk he must have. Kindly direct me to the courtyard. I will take him for a walk myself.'

Fred was still in a state of mild shock when

he shut the courtyard gate behind the pair of them five minutes later.

'I *tried* to stop him,' he told a thrush that had flown down to drink from the fountain. 'I said he ought to tell Hawk-Eye, but he wouldn't. How'm I supposed to stop the Emperor doing what he wants to, you tell me that!'

The thrush chirped and fluttered on to the courtyard wall.

'You're right. If anything happens to him, I've got about as much future as a gruckle,' Fred summed up. 'And don't ask what *could* happen to him on a short walk. This is the Emperor we're talking about, mate.'

The thrush put its head on one side, swelled its chest and launched into song.

'Right again,' said Fred gloomily. 'Anything could happen. I wonder if he's on his way back yet? I think I'll open the gate and have a look . . .'

Half an hour later, he was still looking. Carl's voice from the courtyard almost gave him a heart attack.

'Hey, Fred! You seen the Emperor anywhere? His nibs needs him to sign something and nobody knows where he is. He's not out here with you, is he?'

Fred shook his head.

'Didn't think so,' Carl said cheerfully. 'Dunno why the old bird said to ask you in particular. See you later.'

Heading back along the corridor, Carl thought that his friend was looking worried. No wonder, really, if he'd heard about the messenger and the gruckles. Even Fred was going to find it hard to talk his way out of that.

For once, Carl was wrong, however. Gruckles were the least of Fred's worries as he shot out through the courtyard gate into the street.

The Emperor's fifteen-minute walk had lasted half an hour. Surely, *surely*, he must be in sight?

Fred peered right. He peered left. He peered up at the clouds and down at the gutter. No matter which way he peered, the result was still the same.

There was no sign of the Emperor or the dog.

The city had swallowed them up.

Chapter Eight

Fred slammed the gate and tore down the street. He screeched to a halt when he spotted a woman scrubbing her doorstep.

'Have you seen a man with a dog?' he panted. 'Came this way about fifteen minutes ago?'

She stopped scrubbing to glare. 'Dogs! Filthy beasts! Doing you-know-what on my step.' She gave the step a vicious scrub. 'It's the owners I blame, mind. And so I told him.'

'Oh no!' Fred croaked. 'You didn't!'

'Would you believe he pretended he didn't understand what I was on about? Waste of time talking to some folk. So I picked up my bucket and emptied it over the two of them.'

Struck dumb, all Fred could do was goggle at her in horror.

'That sorted them out,' she went on with

relish. 'Never seen a dog move so fast. Or a man either.'

Fred gulped, and found his voice. 'Which way did they go?'

She dumped the scrubbing brush back in the bucket. 'That way.' She jerked her head towards the city. 'And good riddance!' she snarled as she vanished inside.

Fred stared at the door, trying to imagine the Emperor being tugged at high speed through the streets of the city, dripping wet. A man who thought a ride in his car was exercise! A man who thought you needed gloves to stroke a dog! Would he survive the shock?

'Let him be all right!' he prayed, breaking into a run. 'I'll never complain about stupid jobs again. I'll pull up every daisy. I'll . . . I'll ask for *smaller* grass clippers. Only *please* don't let anything else happen to him. And please let me find him soon.'

Like a small wet tornado, Scruff tore through the city streets.

Like a large wet tornado, the Emperor followed.

Dust from alleys and gardens swirled out and over him. Mud from puddles splashed up and spattered him. A gust of feathers blew out through the door of a poultry shop and stuck to him. Cats spat and hissed. Cars swerved, tyres screeching. A parrot in a cage on a window-sill shrieked with mirth.

Soon they had left the broad avenues far behind. The buildings grew higher, the streets narrower and darker. The Emperor did not know this city.

Scruff did, though: he barked with joy and ran faster, faster, faster – until he raced round a corner and tripped up a woman with a basket. Down on all fours on the cobbles, she found herself nose to nose with Scruff.

Now, where have I seen you before? he wondered. *Give me half a tick: I never forget a smell.*

Unfortunately for the Emperor, Mrs Hubble didn't need even half a tick to recognise Scruff. She picked herself up off the pavement and gave the Emperor a look the like of which had never come his way before.

'*Your* dog, is he? Right! I've waited a good

few days for this. Take that!' The Emperor ducked as she swung her umbrella, but he wasn't in time. 'And that! And that! And—'

Without so much as stopping to wonder if it was the correct thing to do, the Emperor grabbed Scruff's lead and fled.

Mrs Hubble ran after him. 'Stop thief! Your dog's had more of my lamb chops than I have. Stop thief!'

A pack of ragged children playing football in an alley took up the cry. 'Stop thief! There he goes!'

As usual at that time of day, Alf Fishguard was loitering outside the betting shop two streets away. He looked up when he heard the shouting. He didn't recognise the man who was belting up the street towards him, but of course he recognised the dog.

As the Emperor sped past, Alf stepped out of the doorway and grabbed his collar. 'Got you!' he growled. 'You owe me a new pair of trousers, you and your stupid dog. What d'you say to that?'

'I've never met you before in my life!' The Emperor heard the sound of many feet pounding up the next street. He squirmed frantically. 'But if I owe you anything, I'll pay.' He heaved a sigh of relief as the maniac in the green cap let go. 'Ask at the palace tomorrow,' he cried over his shoulder as he took to his heels. 'They'll settle everything. Good morning!'

Alf Fishguard let out a bellow as the Emperor's coat slipped through his fingers. 'The palace? That's where you live, is it? What d'you think I am, some kind of idiot? Come back here! Stop thief!'

The Emperor fled down the street and

darted through a handy gap in a hedge. He found himself racing across a backyard booby-trapped with clothes-lines. He tried to stop, but he couldn't.

'Hey! Where d'you think you're taking my washing?' a woman yelled from her kitchen window. 'Stop thief!'

Take my advice, and don't, Scruff urged.

Trailing one clothes-line, two petticoats and two striped flannel sheets, they pelted on.

'Stop complaining,' Anna told Sam sternly. 'You wouldn't be on a lead if you hadn't got up to tricks yesterday. You're not slipping off on your own this time. We're going to see Mr Gruber and Auntie Hannah, and then we're going straight home. Is that clear?'

Sam drooped. The rope tied to his collar would have stopped a charging rhinoceros in its tracks, and Anna had wound the end round her hand twice. Something told Sam she wasn't going to let go.

'And since you're on a lead, you might as well learn some manners,' Anna said thoughtfully. 'I know you can beg, but you ought to be able to do more. You're not a puppy now. Aunt Hannah says her friend's poodle can sit when it's told. All she has to say is SIT!'

You only had to ask, Sam thought as he sat.

Anna blinked. 'Good dog!' she said, recovering from the shock. 'You picked that up really well. Now, what can I teach you next?'

How to get off a lead? Sam looked at her hopefully.

Suddenly a terrific commotion started up in the next street. 'Uh-oh! Who's in trouble this time, I wonder? At least it's not you for once, Scruff. Let's go and see what's happening.'

Something tells me this is a mistake, Sam thought uneasily. *All right! I'm coming!*

They swung into Halibut Alley.

The crowd chasing Scruff and the Emperor picked up new members on every corner. At the front was Alf Fishguard, alongside the owner of the washing and half-a-dozen of her friends and relations. Then came a policeman, a couple of shop-keepers, a swarm of children, a man selling hot-dogs and a local reporter.

Some way behind the rest, Mrs Hubble tottered towards the wall at the corner of Halibut Alley, to rest and catch her breath. Sam and Anna careered out of the alley at just the wrong moment.

'Whoof!' Mrs Hubble said, finding herself on all fours on the cobbles for the second time in ten minutes. 'Look where you're going, can't you— Hey!' she caught sight of Sam. 'HEY! How'd you get back here, you little varmint, with half the city chasing you?'

Madam, I've never seen you before in my life!

'They can't have been chasing him,' Anna said dismayed. 'He hasn't been out of my sight all morning, Mrs Hubble, honest.'

I'll vouch for that.

'A likely story!' Mrs Hubble picked herself up angrily. 'Stay right where you are, young lady. There's a lot of people want a word or two with you. Hey!' she yelled as Anna beat a hasty retreat back up the alley. 'Come back here, the pair of you. Stop thief!'

Here we go again . . .

'Make for the sewer, Scruff!' Anna cried, feet flying. 'And RUN!'

*

112

The Emperor's trail couldn't have been easier to follow. That was the good news. The bad news was that, so far as Fred could see, in less than half an hour he'd managed to get himself soaked to the skin, attacked with an umbrella, half-strangled, covered in chicken feathers, and mixed up with somebody's weekly wash. How much trouble could one man and one dog get into, he asked himself, following the shouts of 'Stop thief!' into the maze of alleys beside the river.

At least he was catching up. The shouts were just a little ahead and to his right. Or were they to his left?

Funny really, the way the shouts seemed to come from both directions.

Funny? Fred woke up with a jolt. Not funny, serious.

If they were chasing the Emperor from the right, *and* from the left, and he was in the middle . . .

'He's trapped!' Fred cried. 'No matter which way he goes, they'll get him!' He galloped down the nearest alley like a madman. 'Just let me find him first, and I'll never ask for anything ag—'

The prayer died on his lips as a small dog raced past the far end of the alley, closely followed by a large man. The man was limping faster than Fred had seen anyone limp before, especially wearing a clothes-line and two flannel sheets.

'Hey!' Fred shouted, throwing caution to the winds. 'Wait a minute! It's me!'

Can't stop, mate. Got an urgent appointment with a sewer.

The Emperor threw a hunted look over his shoulder, and dived into a clump of bushes by the river. A split second later, an identical small dog raced past the alley from the opposite direction, neck-and-neck with someone Fred had never seen before.

'Hey!' Fred shouted again. 'Your dogginess! Wait!'

Sorry, can't wait – I've just seen my long-lost brother.

Without a moment's hesitation, dog and girl vanished into the bushes.

By the time Fred reached the street, it was full of excited people. They gathered in a dense mass around the bushes where the fugitives had vanished.

'After them!' roared the crowd, but he noticed with relief that most of them seemed a lot keener on shouting than chasing.

'That there's a sewer,' the hot-dog man pointed out. 'Can't go down there. There's germs and stuff. You'll catch something.'

There was a buzz of agreement. Someone put forward the proposition that if you didn't catch something, something would catch *you*.

'Yeah. There's rats and fings,' a youth said knowledgeably.

'And alligators.'

'Hundreds of them.'

'People flush them down toilets.'

Alf Fishguard hesitated. Then: 'Don't believe a word of it,' he said. 'I'm going after him, alligators or no. No one treats *me* like a fool.' He crouched down at the mouth of the pipe.

Fred flung himself forward. 'Wait! You mustn't! There's not just alligators and rats down there, there's something much worse! There's . . . there's—'

Something exploded inside Fred's skull. It might have been the effect of too much rushing about on an empty stomach, but it felt like a brainwave.

It *had* to be a brainwave. Anything less and he was sunk.

He took a deep breath, crossed his fingers behind his back and said: 'There's *gruckles* down there. Big ones!'

Alf Fishguard stood up frowning. 'Gruckles? What you on about, lad? I never heard of no such creature.'

'You're not meant to know about them.' Fred lowered his voice to a whisper. The crowd huddled closer. 'If it gets out, there'll be panic.'

A babble of questions broke out. 'If *what* got out?'

'From *where*?'

'The gruckles!' the ice-cream man shouted before Fred opened his mouth. 'They're down there, in the sewer! Dozens of 'em!'

'God help us all,' said Mrs Hubble, looking grave.

'Why don't they do something about them?' demanded the owner of the clothes-line, looking at Fred.

Luckily he'd had time to work out the

answer to that one. 'Because you can't tackle gruckles without gruckle hounds, and there are only two left in the world. The Emperor had them brought here secretly as puppies last year, and they've been undergoing intensive training ever since.'

'Don't believe a word,' Alf Fishguard said again. He didn't seem so keen to rush down the pipe, though. 'Who's been training them? You, you little whippersnapper?'

Fred gave him a cold look. 'One went to the palace, to be reared under the eye of the Emperor—'

'God bless him!' Mrs Hubble cried, loyal to the core.

'—and the other went to a . . . a secret destination not a million miles from here, to grow up unrecognised in your midst, sort of thing.' Fred wiped his forehead and ploughed on. 'And this very day, the first stage of the battle against the gruckles has begun. At eleven o'clock – which is when your gruckle likes a bit of a nap – the Emperor gave the signal. You saw him lead his trusty hound into the city. At the same time, the second hound was brought here by its gallant owner—'

'You meantersay that chap with the feathers was the *Emperor*?' Fishguard rubbed his chin. 'He did say summat about the palace, but I didn't believe a word of it.'

'You never believe a word of nothing,' said the hot-dog seller severely. 'Let this be a lesson to you. Fancy not believing your own Emperor, what's doing battle with wicious gruckles this minute, to save us all.'

'God bless his soul.' Overcome with emotion, Mrs Hubble reached up her sleeve for an enormous hanky. 'And hers too, poor snippet. Never would I have grudged that dog a lamb chop if I'd known. As for you—' she poked Alf Fishguard with her umbrella, 'carrying on something shocking about a nip in the backside, you ought to be ashamed. What's trousers when the Emperor's life's at stake, and him so fat and all?'

'Not *fat*,' said another loyal subject. 'Not fat as such. More sort of well-covered. And he's got ever such nice eyes.'

'Yes, well,' Fred said, feeling dizzy, 'the point is that I've come from the palace to see how the battle's going, so if you'll excuse me, I'll nip down and see who's winning. If I'm not out in half-an-hour, it means the gruckles have got me, and you can tell Carl he was right, and I should never have done it. He'll know what you mean.'

With a gallant wave Fred crawled rapidly into the sewer.

Chapter Nine

Far beneath the city streets a series of reunions took place.

Here I am! Scruff hurled himself at Anna, hysterical with relief and delight. He licked her nose, her ears, her cheeks and was in every particular so unmistakably Scruff that she dropped Sam's rope to hug her own dog tight.

The Emperor let go of the golden lead and sat down. He didn't look like an Emperor, or feel like an Emperor. He felt confused and very, very tired.

Suddenly, out of the blackness, came a single bark. *Er – excuse me?*

The Emperor looked up.

Something hurled itself into his lap. It was small, solid, and smelly. It licked his nose, his chin, his ear, and generally behaved in a way so unlike the last of the gruckle hounds that

it was nothing short of a miracle that the Emperor knew at once, without a shadow of doubt, that that was what it was. He smiled and (without even having to consult his notebook) stroked Sam's head again and again and again.

There, five minutes later, Fred found him.

There was nothing for it but to tell the whole story, from the fateful moment he tripped over Sam on the palace steps.

When he'd made a clean breast of everything, even the fleas and the plague of gruckles in the city's sewage system, he gave a great sigh of relief. 'That's it, your highness. I'm really, really sorry.' He hung his head and waited for the storm to break.

The Emperor went on stroking Sam's head. 'So my dog is not the last of the gruckle hounds? He's not the last of anything?'

Fred couldn't believe how calmly he was taking it. 'I'm afraid not,' he said, more guilty than ever.

'Who cares?' Fred and the Emperor jumped as a gruff voice spoke suddenly from the gloom. 'Who cares if he's not the last of something?'

'I beg your pardon?' the Emperor said.

Anna scowled fondly down at the dog in her arms. 'Scruff's not the last of anything, and I'm glad he's not,' she said. 'I want him just the way he is. He may not like Mozart or know how to lead a parade, but he's brave and he's clever and he's mine and I love him. I'm not the last of anything either, but you know what my father says?'

The Emperor smiled. He was holding Sam very close. 'What does your father say?'

'It's better to be the first of something,' Anna said simply.

She's right!

Of course she is!

Fred blinked in surprise. 'Do you know, that's what my gran always says. Think of tomorrow, not yesterday.'

'Don't look where you've been, look where you're going!'

'It's what comes *next* that counts!'

'Did she say that before or after the steam-roller accident?' the Emperor asked mildly. 'No, never mind.' Fred blushed as the Emperor got stiffly to his feet. 'Your grandmother was right.' He smiled at Anna.

'And so is your father. Here we are, two dogs and three people: the first of goodness-knows-what. It's time to think of tomorrow.'

Not to mention dinner.

I hope you didn't interfere with my bone?

The next day: 'Read all about it,' the paper boys shouted in the city streets.

'Emperor, children and dogs save city from gruckles!

Statue to be erected to the first of the gruckle hounds!

Gregory the tinker becomes Emperor's special advisor on recycling!

Youngest head gardener ever declares palace garden a nature reserve!

All stray dogs, cats and pigeons to get one free meal a day from palace kitchens!

Long live the Emperor, and long live the Emperor's dog!'

P.S. The first of the gruckle hounds still marches in parades and sits with his head on one side during the Emperor's concerts. He also chases balls in the courtyard and excavates mysterious holes in the Imperial

Nature Reserve which is Fred's pride and joy. Each afternoon he takes a walk with the Emperor. They know every corner of the city now, and Mrs Hubble and Alf Fishguard aren't the only people who say hello when they pass by, or wish them well. At night the golden kennel is empty. Sam sleeps on the Emperor's bed. Neither of them would have it any other way.

Lord Hawk does not approve, but he keeps his mouth shut: these days, the Emperor only has to say innocently, 'Tell us about your last gruckle hunt, Hawk,' to turn his chief advisor dumb as an oyster. Now and then the Emperor suggests Lord Hawk gets his portrait painted in full gruckle-hunting gear, or adds three gruckles rampant to the Hawk coat of arms – but he's a kindly man, so he doesn't do it often.

Once a month, maybe.

Albert and the cat turn up on the palace steps without fail each day for their free dinner. Sometimes Scruff comes too. Not because he's hungry – now Gregory runs the city recycling centre, food isn't so scarce as it used to be when his main preoccupation was recycling Mrs Hubble's lamb chops. He goes to keep his friends company, and to visit his brother.

The messenger has looked for gruckles in every corner of the globe, from Sydney to Toronto. So far he hasn't found any, but his last telegram said he'd had a tip off there was a gruckle hiding out on the fifth floor of the Miami Hilton, and he was going to stay there until he found it.

He's probably still looking.

Last but not least, Scruff still hates Anna's violin so once a week she comes to the palace to play for Sam and the Emperor instead. They think she's getting better.

Honestly.

And they all lived happily ever after.